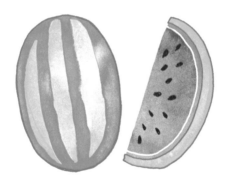

This book belongs to

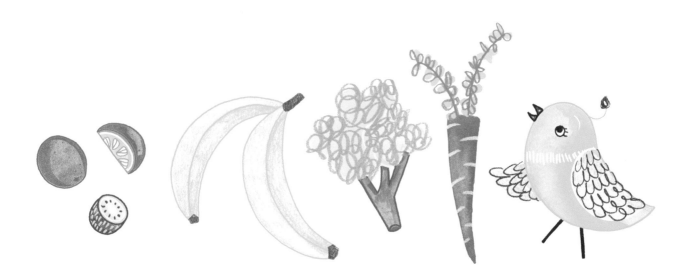

For little Ness and the real Lola Rose

Many thanks to the Home-Start Levenmouth family group who helped me write this story: Nicola Aitken, Pauline Campbell, Kim Graham, Vicky Hynes, Paula McCulloch, Stephanie Muir, Michaela Murdoch, Stacey Rennie-Paterson, Demi Shields, Lisa Small and Lauren Weir. Thanks also for great support from Kate Caldwell, Catriona Wallace, Kay McLeary, Mary Gibbon, Margaret Laing, Stephanie O'Donnell and Eileen Cant.

L. R.

For Mum

With special thanks to Hannah, Dave and Bob for all their support.
Also thanks to Lindsey Fraser, Paula Burgess and everyone at Scottish Book Trust.

E.M.

First published in 2014 by
Scottish Book Trust
55 High St, Edinburgh EH1 1SR

© Crown copyright 2014
Text by Lynne Rickards
Illustrations by Eilidh Muldoon

We are pleased to acknowledge the support of the Scottish Government in the production of this book.

Printed and bound by Belmont Press, Northampton

Never BITE a Tiger on the Nose!

Lynne Rickards

illustrated by Eilidh Muldoon

Scottish Book Trust
inspiring readers and writers

Never bite a tiger on the nose, Lola Rose.
You shouldn't chew that scary
orange creature!

Pick an **orange**
off a tree,

peel it open
and you'll see,

that an orange fruit
is juicier and sweeter.

You mustn't pull a rabbit from his hole, Leopold.
He's not the sort of lunch you want to eat.

But you can pull
up a **carrot** –
if you chop it
you can share it.

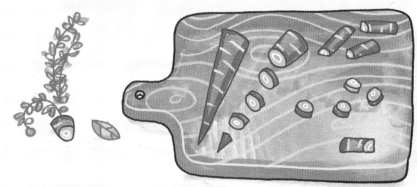

Then you both can have a yummy,
crunchy treat!

You shouldn't chomp an alligator's tail, Abigail.
It's not a very clever sort of snack.

Set that alligator free!
Try a bite of **broccoli.**
It's delicious and will
never bite you back!

You mustn't dip that monkey
in your drink, Humperdink.
He wouldn't play a trick
like that on you.

Why not go and ask Alana
if she'll give you a **banana**?
If you're lucky she might even give you two!

An elephant is much
too hard to chew, Emmylou.
His skin is thick
and wrinkly, like leather.

Though a **melon's**
round and rough,
and its skin is
just as tough,

what's inside is something
different altogether!

A warthog isn't meant to be dessert, Ethelbert.
He's muddy and he's moody and he's hairy.

If you're hungry, in a hurry,
well, a **kiwi's** brown and furry,
and unlike a warthog, not the least bit scary.

You've tried to eat some loopy things for lunch, you silly bunch. But here is where the crazy eating ends.

Take a
picnic
to the zoo –
that's a better
thing to do.

ZOO

Now you've lots of treats **to share with all your friends!**

Lynne Rickards was born in Canada but has been happily settled in Glasgow for many years. She grew up reading Doctor Seuss and A.A. Milne, so she loves to write in rhyme. This is her tenth picture book, and her first written collaboratively. She had a brilliant time working with the Home-Start group in Methil as Early Years Writer in Residence.

www.lynnerickards.co.uk

Eilidh Muldoon loves drawing, gaining a Master of Fine Arts in Illustration from Edinburgh College of Art, where she recently returned as Illustrator in Residence. Although this is Eilidh's first picture book she has applied her considerable illustration talent to other creative areas, including a highly successful and beautiful series of prints inspired by Edinburgh, the city she has made her home.

www.eilidhmuldoodles.com